HEATHER AND THE PINK POODLES
by Marion Engle

Illustrations by
Jordi Torres

Spot Illustrations by
Rich Grote

MAGIC ATTIC PRESS

Published by Magic Attic Press.

For more information contact:
Book Editor, Magic Attic Press, 866 Spring Street,
Westbrook, ME 04092-3808

First Edition
Printed in the United States of America
1 2 3 4 5 6 7 8 9 10

Magic Attic Club® is a registered trademark.

Betsy Gould, Publisher
Marva Martin, Art Director
Jay Brady, Managing Editor

Edited by Judit Bodnar
Designed by Cindy Vacek

Engle, Marion
Heather and the Pink Poodles / by Marion Engle:
illustrations by Jordi Torres, spot illustrations by Rich Grote
(Magic Attic Club)
Summary: Heather and the Pink Poodles have just finished singing and the audience is
loudly applauding. Only one more act to beat, and the Poodles go to New York and perform
live on TV! Can the Poodles win and get a chance to meet teen heart throb *Robbie Starbuck*?
ISBN 1-57513-124-2 (hardback) ISBN 1-57513-123-4 (paperback)
ISBN 1-57513-142-0 (library edition hardback)

Library of Congress Cataloging in Publication Data is on file at the Library of Congress

As members of the
MAGIC ATTIC CLUB,
we promise to
be best friends,
share all of our adventures in the attic,
use our imaginations,
have lots of fun together,
and remember—the real magic is in us.

Alison   Keisha

Heather   Megan

Rose

Table of Contents

Prologue

When Alison, Heather, Keisha, and Megan find a golden key buried in the snow, they have no idea that it will change their lives forever. They discover that it belongs to Ellie Goodwin, the owner of an old Victorian house across the street from Alison's. Ellie, grateful when they return the key to her, invites the girls to play in her attic. There they find a steamer trunk filled with wonderful outfits—party dresses, a princess gown, a ballet tutu, cowgirl clothes, and many, many, more. The girls try on some of the costumes and admire their reflections in a tall, gilded mirror nearby. Suddenly they are transported to a new time and place, embarking on the greatest adventure of their lives

After they return to the present and Ellie's attic, they form the Magic Attic Club, promising to tell each other every exciting detail of their future adventures. Then they meet Rose Hopkins, a new girl at school, and invite her to join the club and share their amazing secret.

Chapter One

VOTE FOR HEATHER

"Heather, you should choose the theme for our class Halloween costumes this year," Alison McCann said as the school door swung closed behind her.

"Me?" said Heather Hardin, her voice squeaking with surprise.

"Sure, you're perfect for it," said Keisha Vance. "You always have good ideas, and you're so creative. I bet you'll think up a super theme."

"How come someone gets to decide for the whole

class?" asked Rose Hopkins, looking at the other four members of the Magic Attic Club. When Keisha and Alison gave her a questioning look, she added "I wasn't here last year, remember?"

"Oh, right," Keisha said. "Sometimes I forget you and Heather haven't been in our school all that long."

"You're right, Keish. It seems like we've all been friends our whole lives," Megan Ryder said, giving Rose and Heather a smile that warmed Heather right through the sharp, cool October breeze.

"Everyone in school gets to elect someone to plan the theme for their class Halloween party," Alison explained. "The class with the most creative costumes wins—"

"Pizza from Poppa Pepperoni's!" Keisha cut in, rubbing her stomach.

"Sounds great!" said Rose. "You've got my vote, Heather."

"I hated the theme Noah Cummings stuck us with last year," said Megan with a shudder. "'Your Favorite Nightmare' —gross!"

"But that won first place in the whole school," Heather protested. "So our class will vote for him again, won't they?"

"Some kids will," said Alison. "But if Noah or another boy wins, he'll choose something ugly. Believe me, with three brothers, I can almost guarantee it."

"I heard a couple of girls saying they want more candidates this time, and I agree," Megan added.

Keisha nodded. "So do I. This year I want to wear a pretty costume—even though I did like being the Creature from the Green Lagoon."

"You were a great Creature," Megan said, "with all that fake slime dripping off you."

"It was pretty cool, wasn't it?" Keisha agreed, making a scary face and holding her hands up like claws. "But we all want to do something different this time. And you have to make sure we can, Heather."

The thought of running for anything made Heather queasy. She shook her head. "Why don't one of you do it?"

"Nope," Alison said. "You're the most artistic."

"You're the best, Heather," Megan added. "You can beat Noah."

"Come on, Heather, say yes!" Rose begged.

Heather sighed. All her friends were so sure she could win, and it was hard to keep saying no to them. "Well… okay," she finally agreed.

"All right!" yelled Keisha. Rose reached for Heather's hand and slapped her palm, and the others did the same.

Mrs. Hardin was in the kitchen, her smock smeared with bright streaks of paint. "What's the matter, honey?" she asked Heather. "You look like a lost puppy." Heather explained the theme contest and the election.

"Why don't you want to run?" asked Mrs. Hardin.

"I don't know—I just don't like contests." Heather hesitated a moment, then added, "I mean, what if I lose?"

Her mother gave her an understanding smile. "Well, I think your friends are right— you have lots of good ideas. And even if you don't win, you could still have a good time just being part of it all. Why don't you give it a try?"

Heather felt pulled in two as she went up to her room. Part of her wanted to stay safely in the background. But she loved coming up with ideas and planning activities, and the artist in her wanted to decide the class theme. She knew she'd do a good job if she were elected.

Well, I already agreed to run, she finally told herself. The least I can do is try my best. She began to make a list of ideas that could be fun for everyone.

"Did you pick a theme, Heather?" asked Alison, leaning across her desk as Ms. Austin got ready to open the nominations.

Heather nodded. "How about 'Famous Fairy Tales'? Maybe we could even go as a group—you know, all from the same story? I was thinking about 'Cinderella'. There are five of us, so—"

"It's perfect!" Alison interrupted. "Heather, you're a genius!"

Rose and Megan nodded in agreement, and Keisha

reached over to pat her on the back. Her friends' enthusiasm was catching, and Heather began to feel better about the whole idea of the contest. Secretly she was hoping to go as the fairy godmother, with a wand and lots of glittery stars sprinkled in her hair. But first she had to win the election.

Ms. Austin finally announced the nominees: Noah Cummings, just as Heather and her friends expected, and Heather. When the teacher asked them to step to the front of the room to tell the class their ideas, Heather felt her stomach knot up. She couldn't help being self-conscious with all those eyes watching her. And what if no one but her best friends thought "Famous Fairy Tales" was a good idea?

"Noah," Ms. Austin said, "what theme would you like to propose if you are elected?"

Noah glanced from face to face with a cocky grin. "Um, well, I haven't exactly decided yet. I have two or three super ideas. All I can say right now is you're all going to love it."

A lot of the boys whistled and hooted, but Heather saw other kids frowning.

"Quiet!" Ms. Austin said firmly. She turned to Heather. "Do you have a proposal, Heather?"

"Y-yes," Heather croaked. Rose gave her an encouraging wink, and she managed to tell the class her theme. Some of them groaned.

"I think it would give everyone a real choice—" Heather began.

Brittany whined, "That's for little kids."

"Yeah, that's baby stuff!" Jim shouted.

Alison jumped up from her seat. "No it isn't! Fairy tales have all kinds of animals and ugly monsters and queens in them. If Heather's in charge, we can all dress the way we want."

Right then the lunch bell rang. Opinions were flying thick and fast as everyone headed for the cafeteria. Heather took a deep breath and melted back into her group of friends, glad to be out of the spotlight at last.

The Magic Attic Club began its campaign during lunch.

"You could go as the Three Little Pigs," Megan suggested to three boys who were always hanging out together. She turned to another classmate, who was tall and lanky. "And you'd be a great Big Bad Wolf."

"Or he could be Snow White," Keisha said, with a big grin and a twinkle in her eye, "and you three could be dwarfs—"

All four boys leaped at her, trying to look angry but laughing in spite of themselves.

"You'd be a perfect Sleeping Beauty," Rose told Janie.

Heather hid a grin—Janie spent a lot of time in front

of the mirror in the girls' room.

"Well, I don't know. Maybe," Janie said. But she walked away looking pleased and lost in thought.

By the end of the lunch period, it began to look as if Heather actually had a chance of winning. It just might be worth running after all, she said to herself.

It was Alison who came up with a super-brilliant idea. "I want to make *sure* you're elected," she whispered to Heather with a big grin. As everyone filed back into the classroom, she told them what terrific chocolate chip cookies her mother made. "Remember, my mom's a caterer. If you vote for Heather, you're guaranteed three of the best cookies you'll ever taste."

Chapter TWO

THE
WINNER IS…

B y the next afternoon, Heather was pretty sure she was going to win the election. It would be so great …

"Let me have your attention, class." Ms. Austin's voice snapped Heather out of her daydreaming. "I have just been informed that someone has been promising cookies in exchange for your votes. That is not a fair campaign tactic. Trying to buy votes is illegal in a democratic society like ours."

Heather felt her cheeks burning as she watched Alison

slide down in her seat. Ali looked as if she wanted to melt into the floor.

"Perhaps the person didn't realize it was bribery," Ms. Austin continued in a softer voice. "Regardless, you will forget about the cookies. Vote for the person you think can do the best job. Now, please turn to page forty-three in your math books."

Alison's face was pale when she passed Heather a note a few minutes later. I *didn't mean it like that!* it read.

Heather nodded. She hadn't realized they were doing anything wrong, either. She wrote back: *Don't worry, we'll win anyway.* Alison looked relieved when she read it.

When it was finally time to cast the secret ballots and count the votes, the room buzzed like a hive of bees. Heather's heart thumped as Ms. Austin sorted the slips of paper into two piles. Which was hers? Which was bigger? Why couldn't Ms. Austin hurry up?

"I'm happy to say it was a very close race," said the teacher at last. "Noah is elected chairman of the Halloween committee by two votes."

Heather couldn't move. She felt like her entire body had turned to mud. Her friends had talked her into

running in a campaign she didn't want to enter, and she'd *lost*. She was so embarrassed, so humiliated...

The second the final bell rang, Heather grabbed her book bag and jumped to her feet. As she passed Alison's desk, she hissed, "You and your dumb cookies!" Then she flew out of the room, leaving her friends behind.

When she reached home, Heather dropped her bag in the hall, scribbled a note to her mother, and headed straight out the door. A few minutes later she was standing in Ellie Goodwin's kitchen, trying to catch her breath. A freshly baked apple pie sat on a cooling rack and a pot of cider simmered on the stove, filling the room with the delicious smell of cinnamon and cloves.

"Just the person I wanted to see," said Ellie. "Want to help?" Her arms were covered to the elbows with thick pulp and seeds from the inside of an enormous jack-o-lantern on the newspaper-covered table. She'd finished the crooked mouth and had just begun cutting out the eyes, which looked like they would never match up.

"Um, I can't," Heather mumbled, afraid that if she spoke to anyone now, she'd burst out crying.

Ellie understood, as always. "Maybe when you come downstairs you'll feel like joining me for a slice of pie and a cup of cider."

"Th-that sounds good." Heather choked out the words, then turned and ran to get the attic key from its silver box. She was grateful for the chance to go up to the familiar attic. The old steamer trunk and wardrobe were open, overflowing with colorful costumes in the bright autumn sunlight.

Heather spotted a pink cardigan sweater in the trunk and pulled it out. "It's so soft," she murmured, stroking the sleeves. As she dug through the trunk to find what went with it, she realized she was already beginning to feel a little better. So many exciting adventures had begun at that very spot. Heather found a matching short-sleeved sweater and a gray felt skirt with a pink poodle appliquéd on it and quickly put them on. The silver leash attached to the poodle's collar flashed in the light.

"Perfect," Heather whispered. "I look like I should be in "Happy Days" or "Grease". I guess this adventure must be about the 1950s. Now to find the right shoes..."

A few minutes later, she stood in front of the mirror, saddle shoes and short white socks on her feet, a pink chiffon scarf tied around her ponytail, and a gold chain with a pendant in the shape of a poodle hanging from her neck.

"Omigosh, I look like I'm ready for a date with Fonzie." She spoke out loud as she admired her clothes.

"Who's Fonzie?"

Heather whirled around. A red-haired girl wearing exactly the same outfit was looking at her with curiosity. They were in a huge room with bare wood floors. One wall was entirely covered with mirrors. It looked like a dance studio.

"Um, he's a guy I know," Heather improvised, trying to sound casual.

"Oh," said the girl. Then she introduced herself with a smile. "I'm Jan."

"Hi, Jan. I'm Heather."

"Dan and the boys are bringing in the equipment.

They'll be here any second."

Heather just smiled, wondering what kind of equipment she was talking about.

"Anyway, I'm really glad you could fill in for Cheryl," Jan continued. "With that awful tonsillitis, she can hardly talk, never mind even *trying* to sing."

"Sing?" Heather asked.

"Of course. It's a song my brother wrote called 'Merry-Go-Round.' We need all the practice we can get before tonight."

I'd better find out what's up before I make a mess of things, Heather thought, fingering the silver leash on her skirt. "We're singing tonight?"

"Didn't anyone tell you? We're going to be contestants on live TV—'Russ Watson's Amateur Hour'." The girl's giggle sounded a little nervous.

"You're kidding!" Heather's hands flew to her mouth in panic.

Chapter
Three

THE PINK POODLES

A teenage boy burst into the room. His red hair was a few shades darker than Jan's, but his freckled nose and laughing blue eyes were just like hers. He had to be Jan's brother, Heather decided. Two others boys followed with a couple of drums and a saxophone case.

"Hey, guys," said Jan,

"better set up quick so Heather can start learning the song."

"Sammy, Buddy, can you bring the rest of the drums in?" said Dan. Then he turned to Heather. "Hi. I heard you have a real good voice. Thanks for helping out at the last minute like this."

"Glad to do it," Heather said, and in a way she was. But she'd never thought she was much of a singer— certainly not good enough to perform on some TV show.

"Okay, Pink Poodles, let's get to work." Dan opened his briefcase, pulled out a few papers, and handed a sheet to each girl. "Heather, you sing the top line, where it's marked soprano, and Jan takes the alto. Can you read music?"

Heather nodded. I sure hope I can, she added silently as she glanced at the musical notes dancing up and down on the pages in her hand. To her relief, as she looked at the first line she heard the notes translated into a tune in her head.

"Good. Let's start with the chorus," said Dan,  walking over to the piano in the corner. "I'll play it once, then you try singing along." He played a lilting, swinging melody that immediately appealed to Heather.

Heather took a deep breath and, crossing her fingers, began to sing. "Merry-go-round, a-round and a-round.

Ride the horse, up and down. Now I'm high, now I'm low..." It was easy to hit the notes—most of the time.

"Good," said Dan. "But on 'horse,' it's an E-flat." He hit the note twice on the piano. "Hear it?"

This time Heather got it right. Dan went through the part with her several times, then Jan joined in, singing the harmony. Their voices blended perfectly, Heather's clear, bell-like soprano tones a nice contrast to Jan's mellow lower ones.

It wasn't as easy to get the verses right. The melody was more complicated, and it was harder to stay on key with Buddy noisily setting up his drums and Sammy noodling away on the saxophone. Dan had to sing Heather's part to help her hear the notes. His rich baritone sounded terrific with Jan's voice.

"You should sing with us, Dan," Heather said. "Or you and Jan could do the duet."

"No, thanks," said Dan. "I'll stick to writing the music and playing piano."

A drum roll rumbled through the bare room. "I'm all set up," Buddy announced.

"Okay, now let's try it all the way through with everyone," said Dan. The whole group rehearsed for the next hour or so, singing the song over and over, trying to make each note absolutely perfect. Heather and Jan stood side by side, facing the mirror, swaying a little and snapping their fingers to the beat. Heather was so caught up in learning her part that she didn't pay much attention to how they looked.

Gradually, as she became more confident, she began to feel there was something missing from the act. Compared to the music videos she was used to, it seemed kind of dull to just stand there and sing. She began to move around in time to the music, dipping and swaying, taking a few steps. But when she saw Dan watching her, she stopped. I wish I could go down the hall and try a few things by myself, she thought as she snapped her fingers and sang.

When she felt Dan's eyes on her again at the end of the next verse, Heather realized she'd been dancing again.

"Say, that looks pretty nifty," Dan said.

The Pink Poodles are Jan and Dan's group, not mine, Heather thought. I probably shouldn't say anything. But Jan has a great sense of rhythm. What if we…

"Maybe"—Heather swallowed hard to clear her throat—"it's probably too late to try this, but, well… I thought maybe we could add a few dance steps."

"Sing *and* dance?" asked Jan, surprised. "But Frank Sinatra doesn't dance. Patti Page doesn't dance."

Heather shrugged. "Okay, forget it then."

"No, wait. Show us what you mean, Heather," said Dan.

"Well, we're on a merry-go-round, right? What if we go up and down like we're riding carousel horses? I dip down while Jan's up, then she dips when I come up. Just during the chorus maybe." She demonstrated while she sang a couple of lines.

"Why not try it?" said Jan. Dan nodded, smiling.

It took a while to get the timing right. Sometimes Heather felt as if they were bobbing around like apples in a dunking barrel.

Then they decided to try adding a few twirls. "Now you spin left, Jan," Heather said at one point. "No, I mean right. I mean—" They collided and fell to the floor.

"*You* go left here," Jan said, sitting up and rubbing her thigh.

"Right." Heather started to laugh. "You're right, I'm left, and I'm sorry."

Jan giggled. "First I'm right, then I'm left, then we're both left—and then we're both wrong!"

"You got that right!" Buddy called.

"Do you think we'll learn it all in time?" Heather asked, pushing herself to her knees and dusting off her skirt.

"Sure you will," said Dan. "When it works, it looks great!"

Suddenly Heather realized she was still missing something important. "If we do win tonight, what exactly do we win?" she asked.

"No one told you that, either?" Jan's eyes grew big.

Heather shook her head.

"The first-prize winner," Jan explained breathlessly, "gets to perform on national TV with—can you believe it—only the hottest teen star in the whole country!—Robbie Starbuck himself!"

"Robbie Starbuck?" Heather repeated. Robbie Starbuck, "America's Dreamboat," was still famous even now, in the 1990s, giving concerts that drew huge crowds of all ages. "Wow! We have got to win this contest tonight!"

Chapter

Four

AMATEUR HOUR

eather's right," Dan said, jumping up. "Let's get back to work!"

The Pink Poodles rehearsed until the song was perfect and the girls had their moves down to a T. By the time Jan and Dan's parents arrived to take them to the theater where the *Amateur Hour* was to be televised, Heather was getting a little hoarse and her stomach was growling with hunger.

The boys carefully packed the instruments in the

station wagon. Then Heather squeezed into the backseat with Jan, Buddy, and Sammy. Dan sat in front with his parents. As Heather peered out the window, visions of cheeseburgers and fries danced before her eyes. Finally she asked, "Are there any fast-food places on the way to the theater?"

"You mean a drive-in?" Jan replied. "There aren't any around here."

Heather had no idea what Jan was talking about. Then she remembered her grandmother telling her how much she loved going to drive-in movies with carloads of friends when she was a girl.

"We don't have time to go to the movies, do we? I meant—" Heather stopped short when she saw the strange look on Jan's face.

Oh, no! she thought, Jan must have meant those drive-in restaurants I've seen in 1950s movies. People used to eat in their cars, off little trays attached to the windows. Jan must think I'm cuckoo, talking about going to a movie.

But the boys were laughing. "That was really funny, Heather," Sammy said.

Heather breathed a quiet sigh of relief. She tried to smile as if she'd deliberately made a joke, then said, "I meant, do we have time to stop and eat?"

"I'm starved, too," Dan said. "We're going to our favorite

place, the soda fountain at Woolword's Five and Dime."

A few minutes later they pulled up in front of the big store. Everyone piled out of the car, went inside, and found the soda fountain. A couple of dozen people sat on swivel stools lining the long counter and at wrought-iron tables and chairs. A jukebox in the corner played 45-RPM records. The burgers were thick and juicy, the fries golden brown, and Heather and Dan even found room for hot fudge sundaes for dessert.

To her surprise, Heather discovered that she was more excited than scared. The idea of performing in front of strangers didn't bother her nearly as much as competing in her own classroom, where she knew everyone and everyone knew her.

At the theater a long line of people was already forming outside to get tickets. When the Pink Poodles went to the head of the line and told the usher who they were, he let them right into the lobby. Heather stopped for a moment taking in the shabby carpeting and faded wallpaper, then turned to catch up to the group. Inside were neat rows of hundreds of seats and a stage that looked as big as a football field. She hurried down the aisle.

As soon as all the contestants had arrived, Mr. Freeman, a short, thin man with a clipboard, called them all together and explained how the show would work.

"We'll open with Russ Watson," he said, pointing to an unoccupied desk on one side of the stage, "then go to the first commercial."

When Heather saw several huge TV cameras arranged along the edge of the stage, she began to wonder whether this performance would be as easy as she'd assumed it would be during dinner. But before she had a chance to really worry, she caught sight of a man and woman in an alcove on one side of the stage. The walls were lined with stacks of dog food cans as tall as the people themselves. A black Labrador puppy was bounding all over the set and chasing his tail. The woman caught him just as he was about to knock over the cans.

"Live commercials, too? Cool," Heather whispered.

"Now here's your order of appearance," Mr. Freeman was saying, reading the names of all the contestants and their acts from a list on his clipboard. The Pink Poodles were fifth, and the last act was the Bennett Brothers, two high school kids and a young boy.

"How good can they be?" said Jan. "That little Benny Bennett is probably only in second grade."

Heather replied with a shrug.

Mr. Freeman directed everyone to the big dressing room backstage to get ready. The contestants began checking their hair, makeup, and costumes. Heather watched, fascinated, while the opera singer took off her scarf and pulled big pink rollers out of her hair, then brushed her curls into a perfect pageboy style. She and Jan checked each other's outfits, gave their shoes a quick buffing, and fussed with their scarves, tying and retying them until they were just right.

A short while later, the five Pink Poodles peeked through a slit in the heavy curtain one at a time. Members of the audience were entering and taking their seats. When Heather saw how many people were out there, her dinner bounced around in her stomach for a moment. But when she reminded herself she didn't actually know any of them, she began to feel better.

"Gee, I'm sure glad Dad and Mom are here to root for us," Jan said nervously as she rubbed her palms up and down her skirt.

"Me, too." Dan pushed a few stray hairs away from his sister's face.

Buddy said "Having my family watching makes me more nervous." "Really? " Sammy said, "I don't mind one way or the other."

Suddenly, Mr. Freeman's voice called, "Attention, contestants. I'd like you to meet Mr. Russ Watson."

A hefty middle-aged man with thinning hair and thick, black-framed glasses greeted the group with a smile. One by one, he shook their hands and wished them luck. He sounded like he genuinely meant it. Heather decided he was a very nice person.

Then it was curtain time! The orchestra played the show's theme song, as Russ Watson walked on stage, greeted the audience, and took his place at his desk. He introduced the dog food commercial and the puppy managed to get through it without knocking over a single can.

"And now," Mr. Watson announced, "Mrs. Arda DeZordo will sing an aria from *Carmen*."

Heather thought the soprano had a beautiful voice, but the audience didn't seem very enthusiastic. Maybe not many of them were opera fans. They were much more enthusiastic about the baton-twirling cheerleader who came next.

"We can beat all these acts," Dan said.

"We sure can," Heather agreed. "We're going to knock 'em dead, right guys?" She was surprised at how confident she felt—and how impatient she became while the barbershop quartet sang and the ventriloquist did his act with his goofy-looking dummy. The next commercial seemed five times as long as the first one.

Then Heather heard Russ Watson say, "And now I'm proud to present a group of youngsters with lots of talent. Please welcome the Pink Poodles!"

Suddenly there they were, onstage under the hot, hot lights, the audience invisible in the blackness beyond, with Dan playing the opening notes. Buddy thumped out the beat and Sammy's saxophone soared along with the piano while the girls sang, dipping and twirling in perfect time.

To Heather it seemed like only seconds later when they faded out on the final "Merry-go-round and around and around..." The audience broke into applause before they had quite finished and cheered when they took their bows.

The five Pink Poodles ran offstage, hugging each other and whispering congratulations. "We're going to win! I just know it," they all agreed.

Heather and her friends crept into the wings to watch the last act. The two older Bennett boys stood behind their little brother, humming a bouncy back-up chorus to Benny's incredible solo. His powerful voice boomed out, "You're so fine. Gonna make you mine..."

Heather and Jan stared wide-eyed at each other, astonished. The voice coming from that seven-year-old's throat seemed strong enough to be heard from coast to coast without the magic of television. It filled the huge theater. When the boys finished, the audience went wild.

"Omigosh, we're in trouble," Heather mumbled.

"I think you're right," Jan said, shaking her head in agreement.

"Well, you never know," said Dan, cocking his head and flashing a small quick smile, but he didn't sound very sure of himself.

When the applause finally died down, Russ Watson took center stage and spoke in to the microphone. "I just want to remind you all that first prize is a trip to New York City to appear on *Ed Smith's Showtime*. The act that places second will also go to New York, just in case the winners can't appear." Then he turned toward the wings. "Now, will all you contestants please come back out here."

One by one, the performers filed out and lined up on the stage. Russ Watson walked behind them, holding his hand above each group in turn while the audience voted with their applause.

Heather looked over her shoulder at a large meter that was measuring the audience reaction; a red pointer moved along a scale when the audience clapped, going higher whenever the sound was louder. The Pink Poodles were solidly cheered, but when it was the Bennett Brothers' turn, thunder shook the theater from floor to ceiling. It was no surprise to anyone that the pointer went all the way to the top.

"Boys, you just won yourselves an appearance with Robbie Starbuck, America's Dreamboat, on *Ed Smith's*

Showtime!" Russ Watson announced excitedly. When the cheers died down again, he added, "And the Pink Poodles will go as runners-up!"

The curtain closed and all the contestants left the stage, trying to sound happy as they congratulated the Bennett Brothers. Then The Pink Poodles headed for the dressing room to gather their belongings.

"We lost." Jan's eyes sparkled with tears.

Heather's shoulders slumped. She'd wanted to win just as much as the others. But when she thought about it honestly, she had to admit that little Benny Bennett and his brothers were amazing. They deserved first place.

Still, the Pink Poodles hadn't exactly lost.

"We *are* going to New York," Heather reminded them all. "And at least we'll meet Robbie Starbuck even if we don't perform with him. We won that much, right?"

"You bet," said Dan. "We're still going to *Showtime*. And, hey, who knows what might happen in the big city?"

Jan blinked back her tears, and Buddy and Sammy looked a little more cheerful.

"Get ready, New York," Heather cheered. "Here come the Pink Poodles!"

Chapter

Five

PRACTICE, PRACTICE, PRACTICE,

I thought we'd never get here," Dan said when the station wagon stopped in front of the DeLuxe Theater in New York City.

His father glanced at his watch. "It's been an awfully long drive. You kids must be itching to get out and stretch. Your mother and I will check in to our rooms, but we'll be back in plenty of time to get good seats. Break a leg, everyone!"

A doorman in a gold-braided uniform let the five Pink

Poodles into the theater.

"Wow!" Heather said as she gazed around.

"This is really swanky!" cried Jan.

The lobby was beautiful, with red velvet draped in flowing swags on every wall and plush carpeting covering every inch of floor. Three enormous crystal chandeliers hung over a huge, sweeping staircase that curved up to an equally elegant-looking floor above. When the group stepped into the theater itself, Heather let out a long, low whistle. More swags of velvet adorned the ornately carved balconies, and several more crystal chandeliers sparkled high overhead. The thick-cushioned, richly upholstered seats seemed to stretch for miles before they ended at the stage, where a number of people were rushing around testing microphones, adjusting lights and cameras, and carrying on urgent-looking discussions.

"Gee, can you believe we're going to perform in a place this beautiful?" asked Jan. Then her face fell. "*Might* perform, I mean."

"Are the Bennett Brothers here yet?" Heather asked. She and the other Poodles scanned the auditorium and stage.

"I don't see them," Dan said. "Come on, let's find whoever's in charge." He and Sammy helped Buddy carry the drums down the aisle and up the steps to the stage.

"What do you kids want?" a man wearing a carpenter's belt asked gruffly.

"We're backups in case the Bennett Brothers can't make it," Dan said.

"Talk to Mr. Cooper, the director." When Dan looked at him blankly, he added, "The guy with the clipboard," and jerked his thumb toward the wings.

Mr. Cooper turned out to be much younger than Heather expected a television director would be, with thick, curly hair that flew out in all directions. As he turned from one person to another, juggling all their demands and problems and issuing orders, he kept running his fingers through his hair, the curls moving in one direction, then another.

Heather and her friends waited patiently till he turned to them. Dan hardly had the words "Pink Poodles" out of his mouth before Mr. Cooper said, "Take your stuff up to the dressing rooms first, then find Gary. He's Robbie's stand-in. He'll rehearse with you till the Dreamboat gets here." Heather thought he said "Dreamboat" with a bit of sarcasm. She couldn't tell if he was just frazzled, or if he thought Robbie Starbuck wasn't such hot stuff.

"Excuse me, but what does Gary look like?" she asked politely.

"Blond, skinny, about six feet tall," Mr. Cooper said. "Dressing room C for the boys, D for the girls. Change into your costumes and hustle back down here pronto and get to work." Before he had quite finished the sentence, he turned to a young man across the room. "Joe, get these kids' drums set up over there."

The group hurried backstage as ordered. In contrast to the elegant theater out front, they found bare wood floors, with narrow, creaky stairs leading to dingy, cramped dressing rooms. The once-white paint on the wooden makeup counter was chipped, and a half-dozen rickety metal folding chairs were lavishly decorated with dents and scratches.

"Lovely," Jan said, running her finger along the dusty metal clothing rack.

Heather wrinkled her nose and shrugged. "Never mind," she replied, opening the small suitcase Jan had loaned her. "Let's put on our outfits and find this Gary guy."

A few minutes later, she and Jan met the boys in the hallway. The silver leashes on their skirts flashed as they raced downstairs, where a tall, blond man in his twenties was waiting.

"The Pink Poodles, I presume," he said with a smile after noticing their costumes.

Dan shook his hand and introduced everyone.

"You're Robbie's stand-in?" said Heather, following Gary and the others to a corner where Buddy's drums had been set up next to a piano.

"Only until I get my big break," Gary answered, winking, "and that won't be long. I expect to be a star any day now."

Heather laughed. "I guess you must be a singer."

"And a dancer. And an actor. I do whatever it takes to get a job, and I do it well," Gary answered. "I never toot my own horn, either," he added with a big grin. Then he glanced at Buddy and pointed to the drums. "Adjust them any way you want. Can I see the music for your number, Dan?"

He looked over the sheet music while Heather and Jan sang it for him. In no time, he and Dan had adjusted the lyrics for a male singer so that Robbie Starbuck could perform the song with the girls. Then Gary sang with them to make sure the changes in lyrics worked. He followed along with the dance steps at the same time, missing only a couple of moves. Heather was amazed at how quickly he had picked it all up.

"Look, Robbie won't have much time to work on this," Gary said. "Let's make the moves a little simpler, okay?"

"Sure," Heather answered. "How about if you do just the dips, and leave the spins to Jan and me?"

"Let's give it a try and find out," said Gary.

The group went over the routine again and again.
Throughout the rehearsal, Heather kept an eye on all the
activity around her. Other acts were practicing in various
parts of the auditorium, but she didn't see the Bennett
Brothers anywhere. They should have arrived more than
an hour ago, she thought. With every minute that passed,
her hopes rose higher. But again and again, she told
herself it was too soon to get excited.

Heather did notice a man in a gray felt hat and gray
coat in one of the front rows. His shrewd eyes followed
the Poodles' every move. When they stopped for a break,

Heather asked Gary if he knew who the man was.

"Sure do," he answered. "That's Mr. Fordham. He's Robbie's manager. He's always looking for new acts to handle. If he likes the Poodles—who knows, he just might sign you up. You could get bookings all over town. Maybe all over the country!"

"All over the country?" The words echoed in Heather's mind, and she felt goose bumps break out along her arms.

Chapter

Six

AMERICA'S DREAMBOAT

hat do you mean Robbie Starbuck will be here 'any minute'?" Ed Smith shouted to the men who hovered around him. "He's the main attraction tonight. Without him, we don't have a show!"

"He'll be here, Ed," said Mr. Cooper, running his fingers through his hair. "He's always reliable."

"I want him here now!" Mr. Smith bellowed.

His wish was granted. The backstage door flew open and the cutest man Heather ever saw dashed in. A flock of girls flowed in right behind him, screaming, "Robbie, please just touch my hand!", "Robbie, if you don't give me your autograph, I'll just die! One hair is all I want, Robbie. Just one hair from your gorgeous head."

"Later, girls, later," Robbie said, trying to free himself from them. "I have to get ready for the show now."

"Robbie, Robbie, Robbie," they screamed. "Please, please, please…"

"How did all these girls get in here?" Ed Smith shouted. "They have to get out of this area—now!"

Some crew members rushed toward the group of girls. A few ran back out the door with frightened looks. The rest scattered in all directions—toward the stairs, the cameras, the curtain. It took ten minutes to round them all up and take them outside.

"Whew! Thanks, everybody," Robbie Starbuck said to the group now clustered around him. "They spotted me coming out of the hotel and I couldn't shake them loose."

"Okay," said Ed Smith. "Now can we get this show on the road? Which ones are the Bennett Brothers?"

"They're not here yet," Mr. Cooper

told him. "But the Pink Poodles are. They've been working with Gary, and they're a terrific substitute."

Mr. Smith mumbled something under his breath and glanced at the clock. "I'll give the Bennetts exactly half an hour. Then we go with the Poodles. Robbie, you'd better start going over your number with them right away."

It wouldn't be long before the Pink Poodles knew whether they'd appear on national television or not. Heather felt her pulse racing as Gary and the group gathered at the piano to perform their number for Robbie. She had trouble keeping her mind on the act and almost missed one of her spins, barely managing to recover.

"That's terrific!" Robbie said when they'd finished. "It's a nifty tune and I love the way you do it. Let's get to work on those dance steps." He took Gary's place between Heather and Jan, and they went through the number again. He was a real pro and picked up the whole routine right away.

When they finished, Robbie put his arm around each girl's shoulder and gave her a quick squeeze. Heather wondered if her face had turned as pink as Jan's.

"You were great," Dan said to him.

"No, the song is great," Robbie replied, "and I like the idea of these dance steps, too. They add a lot of pizzazz."

As the group launched into a serious, hardworking rehearsal, Heather noticed the man in the gray fedora

watching them again. But she and
the other Pink Poodles were
more interested in watching
the time, each of them
glancing at the big black-
rimmed clock in the left wing
of the stage. Heather dipped
and spun and sang, her fingers
crossed the whole time, fiercely
hoping the Bennetts wouldn't show up.

   The minutes ticked down. Twenty…fifteen…ten…nine
…eight minutes to go. Then only five…four…
   Suddenly the auditorium doors flew open and three
boys came racing down the aisle to the stage.
   "Oh, no!" Heather blurted out. "It's the—"

Chapter

Seven

SHOWTIME!

Robbie didn't seem to have noticed anything, but as for Heather and the rest of the Pink Poodles....their mouths were turned down and their eyes were sad. Dan's shoulders slumped as he continued playing the piano.

"We were stuck in traffic in the Holland Tunnel," the oldest Bennett boy, Carl, told Mr. Smith. "It was awful. No way to go forward or turn around, no way to call you…"
He stopped to catch his breath.

"Are we too late?" little Benny asked in a quivery voice.

"No, you made it just before the deadline," Ed Smith said. "You still have a little time to rehearse." The Bennetts seemed to go limp, as if they were ready to melt with relief. This show is just as important to the brothers as it is to us, thought Heather.

"Robbie," said Mr. Smith, "step up here and meet the fellows you'll be performing with."

Robbie turned to the Pink Poodles. "Sorry, guys, I have to go. It was fun singing 'Merry-Go-Round,' with you, though. Who wrote it?"

"I did," said Dan. "I've written lots of songs."

"Can I hear a few of them sometime?" Robbie asked.

For a second, Dan's eyes lit up. Then the light went out of them when Mr. Cooper tugged at his sleeve and whispered, "Robbie doesn't have much time to learn a whole new routine, you know." With an apologetic smile, Robbie followed the director and the Bennetts to the rehearsal area.

Dan, Sammy and Buddy silently began taking apart the drum set. Jan sat down on the floor and stared at her feet. Heather fidgeted with her ponytail.

Then suddenly she announced "I'll be back in a few minutes." She ran off, the hard leather soles of her saddle shoes clattering on the wooden floorboards. When she reached the dressing room, she made sure no one was around, then quietly opened a door.

Heather returned to the stage a few minutes later. She

56

looked all around, scanning every face in sight. In the center of the stage, two girls on roller skates were "dancing" to ballet music. For a minute or so, she watched a comedian go over his routine in the wings, with a few crew members as his audience. Behind the sets stored

near the wings, the ladies in Ed Smith's famous chorus line were practicing their high kicks; Heather wondered how they managed not to fall off their tall spiked heels. The Poodles were talking in a corner.

Gary was rehearsing an ad for refrigerators. He held a string of fish he'd supposedly just caught, and Heather heard the actress playing his wife exclaim how glad she was that their new freezer compartment was so roomy. It looked pretty small to Heather, compared to the one her family had.

Finally Heather found the person she was looking for. Her heart was pounding in her ears as she hurried across the stage.

A few minutes later, she joined the Poodles. "Come on, guys," she urged them, "we have someone to see."

"Hi, everyone," Gary said. "I'm really sorry you won't get to be on the show."

"I guess that's the way the cookie crumbles," Dan said with a small smile.

Heather turned to Gary. "Before Robbie had to leave, he said he was interested in hearing Dan's other songs. Do you have time to listen to a couple of them?"

"He did?" Gary said. "Sure. I'm always looking for new material to perform, too. Lead the way."

They all went upstairs and found an empty room where they could sing without competing with the other performers. Heather stood near the door, her hands behind her back, looking over her shoulder from time to time.

There was no piano or drums in the room, but Sammy played his sax while Jan and Dan sang several numbers. Heather wished she could join in, but she didn't know the music. Part of her was content to listen and enjoy their harmony—and part of her could hardly wait for them to finish.

"Say, you guys are really good—and so are all these tunes," Gary said after the group had finished. "I like it all, and I think Robbie will, too."

"I have copies of the songs in my briefcase," Dan said with a sheepish grin. "I brought them—you know—just in case. I'll run and get a set."

"You don't have to," said Heather. "I have one right here." Dan and Jan gaped when she handed Gary a dozen

or so pages of Dan's sheet music.

"And I want your name and number," said a strange voice from the doorway. A huge smile spread across Heather's face as her friends whirled to face the door. Robbie's manager, his hat pushed back on his head, stood waving a sheaf of music at them.

"Mr. Fordham!" said Gary.

"Wh-what's going on?" Dan asked, stuttering. Even he had lost his cool for a change.

"I like your sound, you two" said Mr. Fordham,

pointing to Dan and Jan. Then he looked at Heather. "Sorry, miss. You sing just fine, but the brother and sister could be real dynamite. Especially if you work out a dance routine like you did for 'Merry-Go-Round.' You looking for a manager?'

"We sure are!" Dan said, trying hard to hide his excitement.

"You mean it?" asked Jan. "You want to be our *agent*?"

The man's heels made a little clicking sound on the floor as he walked over to the group. "You haven't shown this material to anyone else, have you?" he asked Dan, giving him a steely look.

"No, sir," Dan answered. "No one but Gary."

"Here's my card: Fordham Talent. Give me a call Monday morning." He handed a business card to Dan and left.

"Can you believe it? It's our big break!" Jan shouted.

"You bet, Janny," said Dan. "We're on our way."

The Pink Poodles' faces were as bright as the sun.

Then Jan frowned. "I still don't understand how…" she began.

The whole group turned to Heather. Suddenly she felt shy and nervous.

"Go ahead, kiddo. You'd better fess up," said Gary.

"Well, when the Bennetts arrived and I knew we couldn't do the show…" Heather stared at the laces of her black-and-white saddle shoes. "I knew you had the sheet music in your briefcase, so… I went into your dressing room and…I-I guess I kind of took a couple of sets. I knew Gary and Robbie liked 'Merry-Go-Round,' and I'd seen Mr. Fordham watching us when we were rehearsing, and…"

Heather looked up. Dan was staring hard at her. She couldn't tell what that look meant, but it started butterflies swooping around in her stomach.

"I-I hope I did the right thing. I mean…"

The other Pink Poodles rushed over, laughing, and hugged her tight, almost knocking her over.

"This is all thanks to you," said Jan, giving Heather an extra hug. "I don't know what would have happened without—"

"Hey, I'm just a stand-in, remember?" Heather said. "You guys are the ones who put it all together."

A voice from the loudspeaker interrupted her: "Ten minutes to air time."

"Omigosh, we can't miss the show," Heather said. "Let's go."

"I almost forgot my commercial!" cried Gary. "See you later," he called over his shoulder as he sped out the door.

The Pink Poodles zipped downstairs and found a place in the wings with some of the other performers. A man Heather hadn't seen before was standing in front of the thick velvet curtain, telling jokes to get the audience warmed up. He pointed to the applause signs beside the stage and had them practice cheering and clapping.

Then a voice called out, "Five, four, three, two …one! Cue cameras!" The on-air sign lit up.

"Hello, America. Welcome to *Ed Smith's Showtime.* Now may I present the one, the only—Ed Smith!"

The host walked onto the stage to enthusiastic applause. "Good evening, folks. We have a wonderful show for you tonight, featuring a young man you might have heard of—Robbie Starbuck."

At the mention of the name, the audience went wild and jumped out of their seats, cheering and screaming. When the noise died down a little, Ed Smith motioned for quiet and said, "Robbie will be singing one of his hit songs in just a moment, after this word from our sponsors."

Gary came out holding up the string of fish for his "wife." Heather thought he was very talented—he was even good at selling refrigerators. She hoped Mr. Fordham really could help him and the Pink Poodles become a success.

After Robbie's solo, Ed Smith introduced the Bennett

Brothers. The audience sat in stunned silence when they heard little Benny's voice. At the end they broke into thunderous applause, whistling and stomping their feet. Heather joined in the cheering. Robbie and the Bennetts sounded absolutely fantastic together.

As they took their bows, Heather realized that her part in this adventure was over. She whispered good-bye to Jan and Dan, then slipped away to the dressing room, stood in front of the mirror, and gazed at the poodle pendant hanging from her neck.

Chapter
Eight

"THE MAGIC WORLD"

S unlight poured in the windows of Ellie's attic Heather took off the saddle shoes, soft pink sweaters, and gray skirt and put on her own jeans and knit shirt. As she returned the outfit to the trunk, she realized the stiff-looking shoes had been a lot more comfortable than she'd expected. She closed the trunk, went downstairs and locked the door to the attic with the golden key. Then she headed for the kitchen.

"Hello, dear." Ellie, knife in hand, looked up from the

pumpkin on the table. "Good timing. Maybe you can save this poor fellow from its brother's terrible fate." She pointed to the first jack-o-lantern, with its lopsided grin and mismatched eyes.

"Actually, I kind of like the first one," Heather said. "But why do you need two?"

"I'm giving a party for my friends and all my students. You and the other girls must come, of course. I just printed out the invitations and put them in the mail this morning." When she saw Heather eyeing the apple pie on the counter, Ellie smiled. "How about a little preview before we get to work? The cider is hot, and that pie is just begging to be cut."

"I'd hate to keep a pie waiting!" Heather said with a grin. "Listen, Ellie, I didn't mean to be rude earlier, but I really didn't feel like talking then."

"That's all right, Heather," the older woman replied, as she took two plates from a cupboard. "We all have times when we need to be alone."

As Heather ladled out the steaming cider into a couple of mugs, she realized that she was ready to talk about what had happened at school. She sat at the table with Ellie and told her about the Halloween contest.

"I still wish I hadn't lost the election—the whole thing was awfully embarrassing. But I guess we did have a lot of fun campaigning. And I can still come up with a really great costume, no matter what awful theme Noah chooses."

"That's true," said Ellie, refilling their mugs. "People who can make the best of things are the real winners in life."

Heather thought of Jan and Dan. First the talent contest, and again when the Bennett Brothers appeared at the theater—twice in a row they'd lost at something that meant an awful lot more than deciding what to wear for Halloween. They'd been disappointed, but they hadn't been discouraged—and neither had she.

As Heather was leaving Ellie's house, she saw Alison raking leaves in her yard. "Hey, Ali," she called, walking quickly across the street. "Listen, I'm really sorry about what I said in school. It wasn't your fault I lost the election. I knew—we all knew—about your cookie idea. We just didn't

realize it looked like we were trying to buy the kids' votes."

"Keisha, Megan, Rose, and I talked about it," Alison said, leaning on her rake. "It was all a big mistake. And don't worry, I know you said that to me only because you were mad about losing to Noah—especially after I was one of the ones who talked you into running."

Heather thought for a moment. "I wasn't mad, exactly. I was more, like, embarrassed or something."

"Well, as long as you're not mad at me now—"

"Of course not," said Heather.

"Then how about helping me with these leaves?" Alison winked and gave Heather a light punch on the shoulder.

"Sorry, friend," Heather said with a laugh, rubbing her arm as if it really hurt, "but I have this sudden need to get home right this minute! Tell you what, though—after you have five or six nice big piles built up, why don't we all come over and jump in them?"

Alison pretended to be outraged. "And ruin all my hard work? Are you kidding?"

"Not even if I promise to tell everyone where I went in Ellie's attic?"

"*Only* if you promise to tell us," Alison said.

"It's a deal," Heather said. The girls slapped palms, and Heather turned toward home, zipping up her jacket against the cool October afternoon.

Diary

Dear Diary,

I really learned something about myself last week. I'm still not an election-type person, but maybe it's not so bad to try for things in front of a bunch of people—at least once in a while.

I have to tell you about the party. When Noah walked into class last Friday he had that "Wait till you see how smart I am" look on his face, so I just knew his ideas had to be *extra* horrible. Keisha looked at me and rolled her eyes. Rose and Ali pretended they were going to throw up, and Megan laid her head on her desk as if she'd passed out. I nearly got in trouble with Ms. Austin again— believe me, it's not easy to laugh that hard without making any noise so the teacher won't catch you!

Right after roll call, Ms. Austin said she

knew we wouldn't get much work done until

Noah announced the theme, and she called

him to the front of the room. Just listen to

what he said, Diary:

"I heard my worthy opponent", (Can you

believe he actually said that?) "campaign on

the issue of freedom of choice. Since she

came so close to beating me, I figure maybe

a lot of you are thinking the same way and

want a lot to choose from. So I think our

theme should be 'The Magic World'.

I clapped as loud as everyone else, and Ms

Austin grinned like the cheshire cat.

The party was today, and it was a blast!

The Magic Attic Club spent hours making a

huge papier-maché pumpkin and glass slipper.

They were so bulky we couldn't carry them,

especially in our fancy ball gowns, and Alison's

father had to drive us to school. Keisha and Ali made everyone laugh with their ugly stepsister act, Rose played a *really mean* stepmother, and Megan was a perfect Cinderella. I *loved* sprinkling fairy dust on everyone, especially on Noah, for helping us win those yummy pizzas.

    We all decided it was our best Halloween ever.

    Love, Me

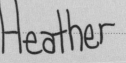

Heather